THE FROG PRINCE

Once upon a time there was a king whose daughter, Princess Goldenhair, was born when he was already quite old. His joy was spoiled soon afterward by the death of his beloved queen.

Happily, the ladies of the court raised Goldenhair with the greatest care. She grew up to become such a beautiful young lady that the sun sometimes paused momentarily in his slow journey around the world to admire her.

Near the palace was a thick forest. Deep in the woods, shaded by a huge lime tree,

there was a well that contained wonderfully clear, refreshing water. Goldenhair often sat near the well in the summer to enjoy the air made cool by the always icy well water.

She was often sad. At such times, she would play with a beautiful golden ball the court jeweller had made especially for her. She would throw it in the air and catch it, her spirits restored by watching the marvelous ball glint and sparkle above her. The ball would often get stuck in the branches of the lime tree. She would then

hold her breath until a breeze would gently blow it to the ground again. Relieved to have it back, she would sigh and cradle the ball close to her body.

One day the princess was feeling very sad because she was even lonelier than usual. She absentmindedly threw her golden ball into the air. It flew at a strange angle and fell straight into the well. Goldenhair could feel her heart pounding. She heard a splash, then silence. She leaned over the edge of the well, but the water was so deep she couldn't even see a glimmer of her ball.

She was so unhappy she just sat down on the grass and wept.

She would never get her ball back! She would never be happy again. No one could rescue it, not even if her father offered a pile of gold as a reward.

Goldenhair cried and cried. The sun watched her from high up in the sky. He wished he could plunge into the well himself and get her ball back, just to see the princess smile again.

Suddenly, a small voice interrupted Goldenhair's sobs. "Why are you so sad, Goldenhair?"

She looked up and saw a big frog sitting on the edge of the well.

"My golden ball fell down the well," she cried. "It's lost forever!"

"I could get it," the frog offered. "That is, if you want me
to."

"Oh, please! I'll give you
anything you want," the princess promised, "clothes, jewels,
anything!"

"I would only want to sit
near you at the table," the frog
said, "and share the food on
your golden plate, and close my
eyes on your soft, warm bed."

Without hesitating Goldenhair agreed to everything he
asked for, thinking only of her
precious ball. The frog dove
straight down into the well and

returned shortly with the ball in his mouth. Sitting on the edge of the well, he lifted his head and offered her the ball. She grabbed it and ran away.

"Goldenhair! Wait!" the frog called after her. "You promised! Don't run away . . ."

The beautiful princess paid no attention to his cries. By the time she reached the palace, the frog was long forgotten.

The frog was as sad as Goldenhair had been earlier. He jumped back into the well, feeling totally alone and discouraged.

The next day, while Goldenhair was sitting at the table with her father and the royal court, the sound of light footsteps filtered in from outside, followed by a familiar small voice.

"Goldenhair, will you open the door?" the voice demanded. "Let me in, you promised!"

She jumped up and opened the door just wide enough to see the same big green frog sitting at the top of the marble staircase. She managed not to scream, quickly slammed the door, and returned to the table, obviously shaken. The king noticed that she was pale.

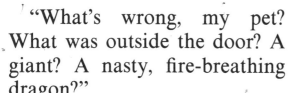

"What's wrong, my pet? What was outside the door? A giant? A nasty, fire-breathing dragon?"

"No, father," she sighed, "just an ugly frog."

"What is a frog doing here at my palace?" the king asked her.

So the princess had to tell the king what had happened at the well the day before. If she had thought that he would understand and approve, she was wrong! She received no sympathy from him. The more she explained, the darker his face became, his frown growing blacker with every second. They all heard the knocking and the small voice at the door again.

"Open the door, Goldenhair, please?" pleaded the frog. "Remember your promise. Open the door."

"A princess never goes back on her word," the king said sternly. "Open the door, Goldenhair, and invite the frog to dinner."

Goldenhair had to do as she was told. As soon as he came in, the frog sprang up onto the princess's chair, took another leap to the table, and started eating some delicious hot soup from Goldenhair's dish. The other guests just watched in amazement. Goldenhair could not force down a single spoonful. The mere sight of the frog destroyed her appetite. If it weren't for her father, she would have taken the frog by the leg and flung it through the window.

The frog finished the soup in no time, ate a good serving of roast beef, even downed a plate of vegetables, and finally polished off a heaping bowl of fruit salad.

"Is there anything else to eat?" the frog asked a passing servant. Learning there was nothing left, the frog patted his swollen belly and leaned back on a corner of the table.

"Well," he said to the princess, "now that I'm full you may carry me upstairs to sleep in your bed, just as you promised."

Goldenhair burst into tears, horrified at the thought of having the frog in her room. One quick look from her father and she knew that she had to go through with it. She took the frog between two fingers and, with a shudder of disgust, carried it upstairs and put it down in a corner, hoping it would leave her alone at last. But as soon as she got into bed she heard the horrid, little voice again.

"Goldenhair, I don't want to sleep on the cold floor," the frog insisted, "I want to sleep between the silk sheets on your bed, where it's nice and warm, just as you promised."

"No, no, no, no, no!" she

shouted. She pulled the quilt over her face and banged her feet against the mattress.

"Even if you don't want me to, I can jump right up into your bed with you," the frog warned, "or should I tell your father that you broke your promise?"

That was it! The frog had gone too far with this princess! That awful creature was not going to get into her bed, and that was that! She jumped out of bed, seized the frog, threw it against the wall, and shouted, "That should shut you up forever!"

What was left of the slimy frog slid down the wall. As the green blob hit the floor, it miraculously turned into a handsome prince.

The princess could not believe her eyes. "Who are you?" she managed to whisper, almost fainting from astonishment.

"As you can see, I'm a prince. A cruel witch put a spell on me, changing me into a frog, a fate I was doomed to suffer until a beautiful princess helped me to escape from the well after throwing in her golden toy. You are that princess! You broke the spell!"

Goldenhair was speechless. She could not believe such a handsome prince could ever have been such an ugly frog!

"Goldenhair," the prince continued, "you saved me from a horrible fate. I fell in love with you as soon as I saw you at the well. I know you love me, too. It is meant to be so. Will you marry me?"

"Well, we will have to ask my father's permission first," the confused princess said shyly. As the surprise wore off, she realized that she loved the handsome prince.

They woke the king in the middle of the night. His initial annoyance quickly turned to

joy when he heard the story. He was delighted to give his daughter in marriage to such a fine and distinguished prince.

"Give me a week to prepare for the wedding," he asked. "This ceremony will be remembered for years to come."

The week flew by. The cooks prepared delicious food, the tailors sewed beautiful clothes, the goldsmiths made fabulous jewels. The wedding ceremony was breathtaking. The celebration feast lasted an entire day and was truly unforgettable.

At dawn the next day, the newlyweds left for their new home in a golden carriage. It had satin cushions and silk curtains, and was pulled by eight splendid snow-white horses. Seated in front was a dashing young coachman, and a footman, the very same age as the prince, stood behind. Richard,

the footman, helped the couple into the carriage and signaled the coachman to set off.

Richard had been in the prince's service since they were both children. When the wicked witch cursed his master, Richard had wrapped iron bands tightly around his chest to prevent his heart from bursting with grief.

As the carriage pulled along, the couple heard a strange noise that sounded like metal breaking. The prince poked his head out the window and asked Richard whether they had just broken a wheel.

"No, Sire," Richard replied, "one of the iron bands around my chest has just snapped."

They heard the noise twice more during the journey as Richard's other two bands snapped. Richard's heart was finally free to beat with joy!

When the coach reached the palace, the young couple were eagerly greeted by the king, who heartily welcomed his son back home. From that day on, everyone lived in peace and happiness.

This is the end of the story.
Now close the book,
turn it upside down,
and you can begin another tale.

where the gypsy had been.

The priest asked the astonished couple to leave the hut with him. He waved his arms when they stood in front of their door. The hut was transformed into a fine palace with a hundred windows. Alexi and his wife were dressed in beautiful garments of silk and velvet.

"Now I know," said the priest, "that only one of the three brothers is truly good and deserves his reward."

The priest disappeared. He returned to heaven and told God everything that had happened.

This is the end of the story.
Now close the book,
turn it upside down,
and you can begin another tale.

For the last time, the angel became a gypsy so that he could visit Alexi and his wife for their test. The angel prayed that they were still good at heart, but he was almost afraid to find out.

He strode through the woods to their hut, knocked at the door and waited. A moment later Alexi opened the door. He was pleased and surprised.

"Look who is here!" he called to his wife. "It's my old friend, the gypsy! You look tired," Alexi remarked to the gypsy, "Come in and rest for a while."

The hut was poor, but cozy and clean. The princess was wearing an old dress but she looked happy and at peace with the world.

They offered their guest what little they had—a jug of fresh water and a fresh-baked cake. The gypsy ate and drank and his sadness slipped away. His eyes sparkled. Alexi and the princess saw a bright flash of light, and the priest they remembered so well was sitting

his heart. He chased the gypsy away empty-handed. The angel instantly became the priest. Shocked, Leo saw the priest wave his arms and everything he had disappeared. It was as if the dairy and the cows had never been there. Leo was crushed.

Sascha showed no gratitude for what he had had. Changing back to a gypsy, he went to find Leo, the middle brother. Leo was happily milking his cows. The dairy business was obviously doing well. The gypsy approached Leo. "I am hungry and thirsty," he begged, "Please let me have some of your milk, in the name of God."

Leo's wealth had hardened

God's name. Sascha sent the gypsy away without a crumb. Now that he was rich, Sascha did not want to give anything away. His money had made him selfish and wicked.

Instantly the angel changed from a gypsy to the priest. A stunned Sascha watched in horror as the priest, with a wave of his arms, made the winery disappear. Water again flowed in the river. To Sascha's great despair everything was as it had been before.

The angel was saddened that

after he appeared at her father's court. Neither of them had ever been interested in wealth or riches. They took pleasure in just being together.

After Alexi's marriage, the angel went back to heaven. When a year had passed, the angel returned to Earth to complete his test. He again appeared as a gypsy and went to see Sascha, who had become fat and self-important.

Repeating the words he spoke when they first had met, the gypsy asked for food in

them, instead, to a hut in the woods.

Alexi and the princess were happy despite the king's treatment. The princess had fallen in love with Alexi's goodness and his handsome face soon

he was with a priest. He struggled with his dilemma and finally thought up a plan. He called Alexi and the two princes before him.

"The first one of you to pick a grape from a dead grape vine will marry my daughter," the king announced. "I will give you each one vine."

One prince sent a messenger to his father seeking help. The other visited a gardener who told him how to care for the vine until it might give fruit again. The instructions were complicated and demanding

and the prince easily lost patience, but he kept trying.

Alexi had been a farmer all his life. He attended to the vine every day, feeding it, coaxing it until it began to show signs of life. Soon it was covered with grapes, while the princes' vines rotted and shriveled.

When Alexi appeared before the king with the grapes from his once-dead vine, the king had no choice but to allow his daughter to marry him. But he was not pleased. He refused to permit the young couple to live in the royal palace and sent

Alexi smiled and declared, "I want a wife who is both good and beautiful."

The priest thought but a moment before he said, "The most beautiful girl, and the most good-natured, is the king's daughter. We will go together to the palace to ask for her hand in marriage."

And so they went, only to learn that two wealthy princes shared his wish and both had spoken with the king. They were each awaiting his reponse.

The king was not impressed with this poor, badly-dressed suitor. He wanted his daughter to marry a rich prince who could give her all the comforts she had always known. But he could not turn Alexi away since

Alexi was quiet for a moment and then spoke softly. "Yes, I will go with you, but first you have to let me know that my brothers are okay. I haven't seen or heard from either of them since they went off with you."

"They are both happy," the priest assured him. "Sascha's winery and Leo's dairy are both doing very well and your brothers are managing fine. I have made their dreams come true." Alexi knew the priest spoke the truth. He sighed in relief at the news, nonetheless, and started to walk with the priest. They had not gone far when the priest stopped and said, "It is now your turn, Alexi. What is your wish?"

peared where there had been none, and a dairy farm materialized nearby, producing butter and cheese.

"All this is yours," the priest told Leo, "but remember to put it to good use." He vanished, leaving a startled Leo to manage his new business. Alexi walked back to the farm alone, a bit sad yet happy for both his brothers. Would he ever see them again, he worried. Would they be all right?

The following morning the priest again came to the field and found Alexi hard at work. "Care to come for a walk?" the priest asked him.

course, came along. They walked until they reached a clearing in the forest. White doves fluttered about, searching for food.

The priest remarked to Leo, "It's very nice here, isn't it?"

"Yes," replied Leo, "but it would be even nicer if those doves were fine milk cows!"

As the words were spoken, the doves became black-and-white cows, a few lambs ap-

Sascha to join him on a walk. The other brothers followed. They came to a halt by the bank of a winding river.

Sascha sat down on a rock and gazed longingly at the water. "Wouldn't it be wonderful if the river ran with wine instead of water?" he murmured.

Suddenly the water changed into foaming red wine, and a working winery appeared nearby. Sascha jumped up and down in excitement while his brothers watched in amazement.

"It is all yours," the priest told Sascha, "but always remember to put it to good use." He disappeared leaving Sascha behind to take care of his new business. His brothers returned to work, happy that Sascha had such good fortune.

The priest returned to the field the next day and invited Leo for a stroll. Alexi, of

On the third morning, the gypsy found Alexi collecting firewood. Again, he requested food, in the name of the Lord, with the same result.

The angel didn't know what to do. He was ready to swear that all three brothers were equally kind and good, but he felt that he had to be absolutely certain before reporting his findings to God. He decided to try another test.

This time the angel appeared as a priest. He returned to the field where the brothers were working together. He invited

find the three brothers.

That morning it was Sascha's turn to work the field, preparing the ground for planting lettuce. The gypsy approached him and, holding his hand out, he begged, "Would you please give me something to eat, praise God?"

"I don't have much to offer you," Sascha answered, "but you're welcome to a pear." He picked the ripest, richest pear he could find and gave it willingly to the gypsy. Thanking him for his kindness, the gypsy left.

The next day was Leo's turn to work in the garden. While he was weeding, the gypsy returned, repeating his request for food. Leo also gave the gypsy a ripe, delicious pear.

tree that stood in the middle of their field. This tree produced the most delicious sweet and juicy pears.

Sascha, Leo and Alexi had to work very hard all day long just to support themselves, but they never complained. They loved each other and were happy with what they had, although sometimes they dreamed of better times and hoped for a bit of good luck.

From up high in heaven, God looked down on the three brothers and was pleased with what He saw. Before rewarding them for their labors, He decided to first test all three of them, and called on one of His angels to help.

"Go down to Earth," God ordered the angel, "and see if those three brothers are really as good as they seem from here."

The angel obeyed at once and flew to Earth. Using his heavenly powers he disguised himself as a gypsy as soon as he landed. He knew that his glorious wings and halo would attract too much attention and ruin the test. Then, he set off to

THE PEAR TREE

Long ago in a far away land there were three brothers named Sascha, Leo and Alexi who were orphaned in their youth. They made a modest living by farming on a small plot of land. The brothers were exceptionally proud of a pear